This Walker book belongs to:

———————————

———————————

———————————

Author's Note:

Trees really can help one another. Trees can send nutrients to each other through a network of fungi in the soil. Trees can send warning signals about environmental change via the same network. Trees can also release a gas into the air to warn other trees of attack by animals or insects. Scientists are just at the beginning of understanding how trees are able to communicate with and support other trees.

For Anne. I will always be thankful for the deep roots of our friendship. **L.G.**

For my granny, who gave me all her love. **P.M.**

First published 2022 by Walker Books Ltd, 87 Vauxhall Walk London SE11 5HJ

This edition published 2023

2 4 6 8 10 9 7 5 3 1

Text © 2022 Laura Gehl • Illustrations © 2022 Patricia Metola

The right of Laura Gehl and Patricia Metola to be identified as author and illustrator respectively of this work has been asserted in accordance with the Copyright, Designs and Patents Act 1988

This book has been typeset in Filosofia

Printed in China

CIP Code: 0124/B2471/A6

British Library Cataloguing in Publication Data: a catalogue record for this book is available from the British Library

ISBN 978-1-5295-1101-7

www.walker.co.uk

APPLE
and
MAGNOLIA

LAURA GEHL and PATRICIA METOLA

WALKER BOOKS
AND SUBSIDIARIES
LONDON · BOSTON · SYDNEY · AUCKLAND

Britta's two favourite trees,
Apple and Magnolia,
were best friends.

Britta couldn't explain how she was
so sure about the friendship, or how
the trees had become best friends
in the first place. But deep down
in her heart, she knew it was true.

Britta visited the trees every day.

She watched Apple
give Magnolia gifts.

And saw Magnolia

wave at Apple.

Britta danced along

as the two trees

swayed together

under the stars.

Dad said, nicely, that
he didn't think trees
could be friends.

Bronwyn said, not as nicely,
that trees absolutely, positively
could not be friends.

But Nana said
unusual friendships can be
the most powerful of all.

Then one day, Magnolia's branches started to droop.

Her bark grew patchy and grey.

Her leaves turned brown instead of yellow.

Dad said, nicely, that he
didn't think Magnolia
would survive the winter.

Bronwyn said, not as nicely,
that Magnolia absolutely,
positively would not
survive the winter.

But Nana asked if Britta
had a plan to help Magnolia.

Britta did.

She tied a string with two cups so
that Apple could hear Magnolia's sighs,
and Magnolia could hear Apple's
sweet whistling songs.

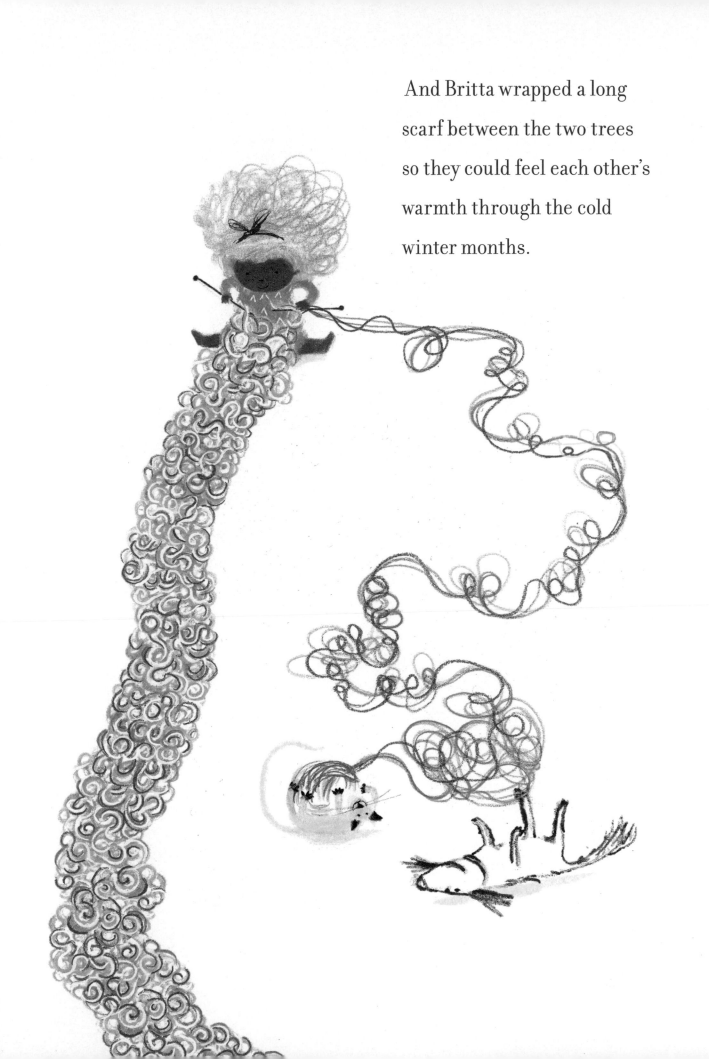

And Britta wrapped a long
scarf between the two trees
so they could feel each other's
warmth through the cold
winter months.

She hung a strand of lights
between Magnolia and Apple,
so they could see each other
even on moonless nights.

One morning Britta looked at the limp string, the sagging scarf, and the drooping lights. Was it her imagination, or were the two trees closer together than they had been before?

Britta measured the distance
between Magnolia and Apple.

Each morning she measured again.

Dad said, nicely, that he didn't think the trees
were growing towards one another.

Bronwyn said, not as nicely, that the trees absolutely,
positively were not growing towards one another.

But Nana helped Britta make a chart.

The measurements were definitely getting smaller.

And deep down in her heart,

Britta felt a seed of hope start to grow.

In the spring, Apple's small pink flowers arrived
right on time.

Magnolia's ... didn't.

But every day, Britta's measurements grew smaller and smaller,
and her hope grew stronger and stronger.

When Magnolia's first blossom appeared,
Britta's hope blossomed, too.

And when hundreds of pink magnolia
flowers burst into bloom at last,
Britta made pink
necklaces for
both trees to
celebrate.

Dad said, nicely, that he didn't think Apple had helped Magnolia survive the winter.

Bronwyn said, not as nicely, that Apple absolutely, positively
had not helped Magnolia survive the winter.

But Nana said unusual
friendships can be the
most powerful of all.

And deep down
in her heart,
Britta knew
it was true.

Dear Reader,

Have you ever spent time around trees? Did being near trees make you feel calmer or happier? Scientists have found that trees make people feel better and can cheer people up if they are sad. I know that is true for me. I live near the woods, and I try to spend time there every single day (even in the rain or snow!).

The holiday of Tu B'Shevat is the New Year of the Trees. Some Jews celebrate this holiday by eating fruits from trees, such as olives, figs, and pomegranates. Many also think of Tu B'Shevat as a day to remember how important it is to take care of our planet.

Just as Apple gives Magnolia gifts in this story (apples, of course!), trees give humans many gifts: shade, oxygen to breathe, and lots of different fruits and nuts. Chocolate comes from trees, too!

On Tu B'Shevat, we can think of ways to thank the trees that give us so much. We might plant new trees, pick up trash, or remember not to waste the paper that comes from trees. (We can draw on both sides of a piece of paper, for example, and re-use magazines to make collages.)

Trees don't have mouths to speak with, but they do send each other messages through the air and underground. If Apple and Magnolia *could* talk, I think they would join me in saying Chag Sameach (Happy Holiday!) to you and your family this Tu B'Shevat.

Your tree-loving friend,

Laura Gehl

Laura Gehl is the author of more than thirty popular picture books, board books, and early readers. Her books include *One Big Pair of Underwear*, the Peep and Egg series, *I Got a Chicken for My Birthday* and *Odd Beasts*. Laura lives in Maryland, USA, with her husband, four children and a large stash of dark chocolate. Find her online at lauragehl.com and on Instagram and Twitter @AuthorLauraGehl.

Of *Apple and Magnolia*, Laura says, "Trees give humans and other animals so much, including oxygen, shade, and fruit, but for me personally the biggest gift from trees is the sense of peace I feel when I am near them. I love that trees give gifts to one another as well as to us, and that is why I wrote this book."

Patricia Metola is an illustrator from Madrid, Spain. After studying Graphic Design, she spent several years working as an art director before focussing on her own illustrations. Since then, she has illustrated more than twenty books and her art has been displayed internationally at the ABC Museum, the Madrid National Library and the Itabashi Art Museum of Japan. *Love from Alfie McPoonst* was her first title with Walker Books. Find her online at patriciametola.blogspot.com.es and on Instagram as @patriciametola.

Of *Apple and Magnolia*, Patricia says: "Apple and Magnolia is a lovely story that connects with my childhood in the countryside with my granny. I still adore plants. I don't crochet scarves for them, but I pamper and talk to them."